WALT DISNEY'S

MICKEY MOUSE

meets

ROBIN HOOD

ABBEVILLE PRESS · PUBLISHERS · NEW YORK

ISBN 0-89659-176-X

ADVENTURES WITH ROBIN HOOD

IT SURE MUST BE! LOOK WHERE THE FLOWER IS NOW—

F'GOSH SAKES! NOW I'VE GOTTA DO SOMETHIN' T' GET IT BACK DOWN AGAIN!

QUICK! GIMME ALL TH' REDUCING PILLS YOU'VE GOT!

AND IF THIS DOESN'T WORK, WHAT AM I GONNA DO!? I'VE GOTTA REDUCE IT A LITTLE AT A TIME—

'CAUSE IF IT EVER TOPPLES OVER, IT'LL BUST TH' HOUSE!

I OUGHTA BE CLEAR UP ON TOP—BUT—WELL THIS IS TH' BEST I CAN DO! HERE GOES!

HOT DOG! IT WORKS!

WHOOPEE! WHAT A DISCOVERY! WITH SOME PRACTICE— I CAN GROW 'EM ANY SIZE!

WHEN I GET THIS ONE DOWN, I'M GONNA PLAY AROUND WITH TH' STUFF!

JUST A FEW MORE SHOTS— AN' IT'LL BE READY TO—

ULP!

OH BOY! LOOK WHAT HAPPENED TO IT—

A SEED!

5-3

PLUTO RUNS AWAY TERRIFIED, WITH THE HUGE FLY IN HOT PURSUIT!

OF ALL TH' SILLY PICKLES T' BE IN! IF I WAS SOMEBODY ELSE I'D PROB'LY BE LAUGHIN' AT ME!

BUT IT'S NO LAUGHIN' MATTER! I GOTTA GET TO TH' BASEMENT AN' GET BIG AGAIN!

GR-RRR-R-RRR!

WUZZ! WUZZ! WOZZ! WOZZ! WOZZ!

ZUZZ YEZ WUZZ, ZOZZ!

WOP!

F' GOSH SAKES! NOW I AM IN A JAM! WITH PLUTO GONE, HOW'LL I EVER GET OFF THIS TABLE?

SOZZ! YUZZ ZOZZ, HUZZ! WOZZ!

!

© 1936, by Walt Disney Enterprises, World rights reserved. 6-14

WHAT A COINCIDENCE! MICKEY IS AMAZED AT HIS GOOD FORTUNE!

THY QUICK WIT SAVED MY LIFE, LAD! NOW I MUST REPAY THEE!

WILT THOU SERVE ME AND ENTER MY COMPANY OF MERRY MEN? WHAT SAYEST THOU?

OH BOY! OH BOY! I SAYEST IT'S SWELL!

HELLO, MY FRIENDS!

LOOK!

'TIS ROBIN HOOD!

HE'S TURNED BEGGAR!

A CLATTERING TIN-SMITH, ON MY HONOR!

CLATTER! KLANK!

WHAT MANNER OF CREATURE IS THIS?

A STRANGE-LOOKING URCHIN!

METHINKS HE IS A FOREIGNER! CANS'T THOU SPEAK?

SURE! I'M A NEW MAN IN YER GANG!

A NEW MAN? HAW! HAW!

I SAY A MERE INFANT!

IF YOU ARE A MAN, LITTLE ONE, I WOULD FAIN TEST THY STRENGTH! SMITE ME ON THE JOWLS!

WELL — IF THAT'S TH' WAY YA WANT T PLAY — O.K. — I'LL DO IT!

SMACK!

SO! AND NOW IT IS MY TURN!

NAY! THOU ASKED FOR IT, METHINKS!

LET TH' BIG PALOOKA COME! I CAN TAKE CARE OF HIM!

VERY WELL! SO BE IT! YOU SHALL FIGHT WITH LONG STAVES! MICKEY MOUSE AND LITTLE JOHN!

LITTLE JOHN! OH GOSH!

WALT DISNEY

6-88

I'VE READ A LOT ABOUT YER GANG, ROBIN HOOD, BUT TH' BOOKS DON'T SAY MUCH ABOUT HOW YA SPEND YER TIME WHEN YER NOT BUSY!

THERE'S ALWAYS PLENTY TO DO!

"FRIAR TUCK AND LITTLE JOHN KEEP TRIM BY ENGAGING IN FRIENDLY BATTLING!"

"OTHERS PARTICIPATE IN ALL MANNER OF SPORTS—SHOOTING, WRESTLING AND JUMPING!"

"WHILE OTHERS FASHION NEW ARROWS, MEND CLOTHES, OR GATHER FIREWOOD!"

AH! BUT COME! NOW IT'S TIME FOR DINNER!

WHONN-N-N-NK!

AS THE NEWEST MEMBER OF OUR BAND, THOU WILT SIT IN THE PLACE OF HONOR—HERE ON MY RIGHT HAND!

WHAT'S TH' IDEA OF TH' BOWS AN' ARROWS?

'TIS SIMPLE, MY FRIEND! IN SHERWOOD FOREST WE HAVE NO SERVANTS TO PASS THE FOOD!

SO A MAN MUST NEEDS GET HIS OWN! HERE—I'LL SHOW YOU HOW TO PASS THE FOOD!

SEE? HERE THOU ART! THE FATTEST PHEASANT ON THE PLATTER!

OH BOY! THIS IS A SWELL WAY T' LIVE!

YES, BUT THOU HAST NOT SEEN THE BEST FUN OF ALL! WAIT TILL YOU SEE OUR REAL SPORT!

WHAT SPORT IS IT?

HOLDING UP AND ROBBING FAT TRAVELLERS ON THE PUBLIC HIGHWAYS!

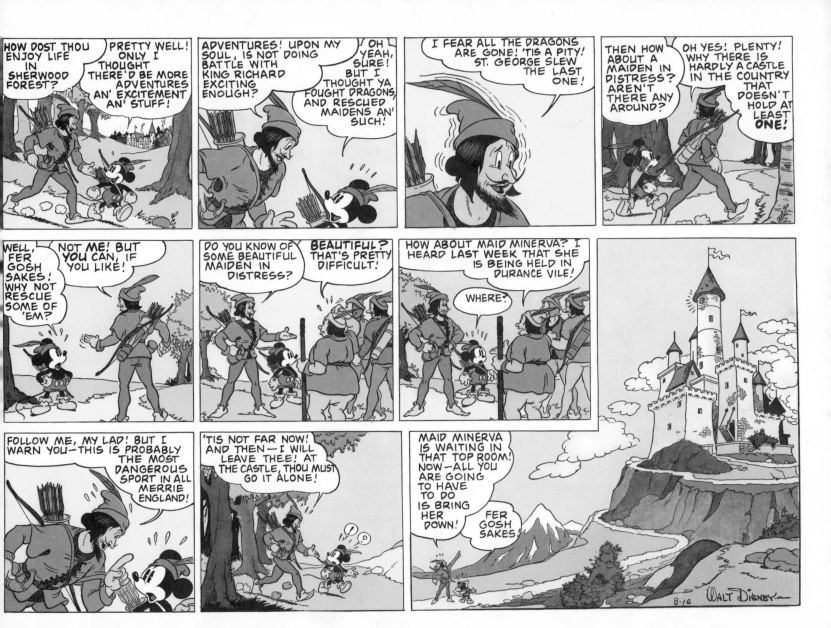

MICKEY BRAZENLY GOES TO THE FRONT DOOR OF THE CASTLE IN ORDER TO RESCUE THE BEAUTIFUL MINERVA!

DEFEND YOUR-SELVES!

WHY SHOULD WE? ARE WE BEING ATTACKED?

I'VE COME HERE TO RESCUE A MAIDEN IN DISTRESS!

OH! WHY DIDN'T YOU SAY SO? I WAS WORRIED THERE FOR A MINUTE!

SIR BAFFLEBRANE WILL SHOW YOU TO HER ROOM! AND IF YOU WANT TO FIGHT ON THE WAY, JUST FOR FUN, HERE IS A SWORD!

YA MEAN YER NOT GONNA STOP ME?

WHY SHOULD WE? I'M SURE MAID MINERVA WOULD BE DELIGHT-ED!

IT IS THIS WAY, MY FRIEND!

I DON'T GET IT! ISN'T SHE IN DISTRESS?

SURE! BUT SHE WAS IN DISTRESS BEFORE SHE CAME HERE!

WHAT ABOUT?

IT'S SIMPLE! SHE WANTS TO GET MARRIED! SO SHE CAME TO STAY IN DURANCE VILE UNTIL SOME SAP WOULD COME ALONG TO RESCUE HER!

Ye Maiden in Distress

WELL GO RIGHT IN!

HEY! WAIT A MINUTE! DO YA MEAN IF I RESCUE HER, SHE'LL WANT T' MARRY ME?

Ye Durance Vile

OF COURSE! YOU HAVE TO MARRY HER! IT'S THE CUSTOM!

TH' CUSTOM BE HANGED!

NOW I KNOW WHY ROBIN HOOD SAID THAT THIS RESCUIN' STUFF WAS SO DANGEROUS!

EITHER RESCUE HER OR ANSWER TO ME!

8-23

WALT DISNEY

96

WHAT A NICE COUPLE!

LISTEN! I'M NOT GONNA MARRY **ANYBODY**—AT LEAST FOR A THOUSAND YEARS! UNDERSTAND?

IT WILL BE EITHER A WEDDING— OR A **FUNERAL** FOR YOU! TAKE THY CHOICE!

UH—WELL—IF YOU PUT IT THAT WAY—

GOODNESS? ISN'T THIS ROMANTIC? A MILITARY WEDDING!

THAT'S SURE TH' **ONLY** WAY IT'S GONNA **BE** A WEDDING!

ART THOU A PRINCE? A DUKE? OR A KNIGHT? OR WHAT?

NONE OF 'EM! I JUST DECIDED I'M AN AWFUL **SUCKER!**

BUT MAYBE WHEN WE GET T' SHERWOOD FOREST— ROBIN HOOD'LL FIX IT FOR ME!

HO MICKEY! I SEE THOU HAST TAKEN THY BRIDE!

BUT, ROBIN—LISTEN! I TELL YA I—

HULLO! COME FORTH MY MERRY MEN! A WEDDING IS IN BLOOM!

GO AHEAD, FRIAR TUCK! LET THE CEREMONY PROCEED!

© 1936, by Walt Disney Enterprises, World rights reserved. 9-13

WALT DISNEY

Coming Attractions

Will Mickey find Captain Church-mouse, survive gruesome tortures, and escape a desert ambush?

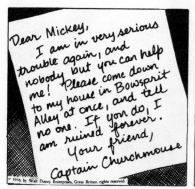

Find out at your nearest book or toy store

Will Donald give up a bag of
gold and a lake of diamonds for
a glass of water?

Find out at your nearest book or toy store

Will Donald find the Golden
Helmet before Azure Blue does and
save America from a tyrant?

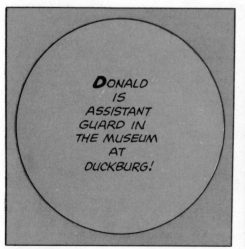

DONALD
IS
ASSISTANT
GUARD IN
THE MUSEUM
AT
DUCKBURG!

Find out at your nearest book or toy store

What will life be like for Mickey and Goofy among sea monsters, cave men, and dinosaurs?

Find out at your nearest book or toy store